SEX CRUMBS3

Jordan Stron

To my Sons,
Michael and Gabriel -

Thanks for giving me a reason to live
through the dark times -
Till all the Stars in Heaven lose their light;
I'll always love you-
Dad.

"Reclaim the footprints from the Sea shores
For each single one tells a story -
A sentient being once stood here
Eternity's secrets locked within their Infinite
blood"

@unix_jim

SEX CRUMBS 3

Jordan Stron

Contents

Preface

Love, Divorce and Redemption

What exactly is "true love" and how do you go about it? Is "True Love" even possible in a world of on-line dating, casual sex, easy access to porn and the consumerism of the marriage act? How do you tell if a Love is genuine or not? Is your partner cheating on you and if Yes, should you cheat in vengeance?

These stories will attempt to spare you the woes of the Love Jungle with first hand recollections of one person's search for Love and its consequences across all four continents.

They are also not a confessional, merely a detailed illustration of cause and effect in the game of love through shared experiences and thence to the final analysis and some answers to today's critical relationship issues namely:

1. Is "True Love" a one-off thing?

2. Are Orgasms overrated?

3. Is Love possible without Sex?

4. Can you be in Love with several partners?

5. Differentiation between lust and love

6. Where exactly is the mythical "G" spot and what do you do once it's discovered?

7. And finally, the answer to the age-old question "What are you thinking?"

I'll share my experiences of how tiny misinterpretations, words left unsaid and awkward moments of pained silences end up needlessly ruining many relationships, along with the impact of self-doubt, external forces and malicious people unwittingly introduced into private situations. "True Love" is a bond that eventually forms between two people willing to make things work despite our human foibles – therein lies the key to true happiness. If learning from my mistakes prevents a single heartbreak then these were tales worth sharing.

Chapter 1

The Remorseful Lothario

After my introduction and conversion to Tantric Sex by the Ladies from Kitchener I soon realized my interest in vengeful sex was not only inane but also self-destructive. I became ashamed of my past encounters and changed phones several times in an effort to avoid my previous "friends with benefits." Eventually I moved to a new Condo on the Lakeshore to avoid unannounced desperados and sex maniacs who couldn't fathom my change of reality and newly found aversion to "fun" and I resumed studying again.

After a year of reckless living I was slowly returning to normal. Sex was now something to cherish and no longer meaningless romps with like-minded tramps. My two "Sex Gurus" eventually saw the change in me and we mutually broke off our threesome and after a month or two without sex it felt like I was awakening from a bad dream - I changed cars for something more professional, got a job that required me to wear a suit and started eating healthy again.

I stopped gambling and mainly kept to myself. Once in a while Lucy would check up on me and we'd go out for a meal – she was now engaged so I had to find myself a new love interest.

I still blamed Dorotka – not only for losing Lucy, but also for shattering my heart into a zillion pieces and turning me into a man-whore version of herself, the witch.

Chapter 2

An Eternal Love - Caley

It was the season of bliss, a summer where Raves, Acid-House, Techno music and the likes of 2Unlimited, C&C and "The Prodigy" reigned supreme on the clubbing scene. I was now a young upstart software programmer with a new flat out west and the latest Audi to my name. Yes, I was still single but I was now reasonably cured from my year of binges and assorted debauchery with pretty faces - I had to find a real girlfriend.

I received a call from my friends Ali and Bobby regarding the upcoming Toronto Island Summer Fest and I promised to pick them up as they lived uptown. I would meet Caley after the rave, on a hot sweltering July evening. I had parked fortuitously on the Lakeshore Boulevard, boarded the ferry to the island and after a day fueled with alcohol and techno music, had returned to my car with my friend Ali. We planned to go for dinner in the Yorkville area which meant changing from our raving gear of sweat-suits and sneakers into something more respectable and therefore emboldened by the alcoholic fumes in our system, decided to change right there behind the car in a city of over four million people.

Needless to say, we were caught with our pants down in full glory mode as two ladies turned the corner midway through our Supermen routine – they hurriedly crossed the street to give us some privacy, giggling and blushing but the damage had already been done. After we'd changed Ali suggested we try picking the ladies up and inviting them to dinner. His logic was very simple – they had already seen us naked anyway so even if they said "no" we couldn't get any more embarrassed.

I therefore turned the car around and pulled up to the still giggling duo and we introduced ourselves. It turned out they had just come from the rave also and were walking into town to catch a bus home so we offered to drive them. And that's how we met the two beauties from Ireland. Their names were Bridgette and Caley.

Bridgette was the elder of the two and lived in Toronto – her sister was visiting her for the summer and had on a French Beret which made her look almost under-aged but her sister assured us she wasn't: she's just short, she teased Caley. They lived mid-town and agreed to have dinner with us but they first needed to go home to shower and change.

Most of the trip was spent talking to Bridgette as her sister was either shy or not interested: we dropped them off home and agreed on an 8pm pickup. We returned to Ali's home to get properly dressed, with a plan to take the girls out to dinner, after which I'd go home if the vibe Ali was picking up from Bridgette was right and he got lucky – we decided Caley was too young and not worth pursuing and that Bridgette was just lying about her age.

We headed to a restaurant in Yorkville and as we'd guessed Bridgette had the hots for Ali - they spent a lot of time walking outside to kiss in an alleyway, leaving Caley and I alone. We were chit chatting politely when Ali called me to the bathroom and begged me to stay with them as he wanted to take Bridgette out dancing and she would not leave her sister alone. Anything for my mate I responded.

We took the ladies to clubland and ended up in Club Oz and that's when the most wonderful of transformations occurred. The minute we got into the Club Ali rushed his new girlfriend onto the dance floor while I did the gentlemanly thing and offered Caley a drink and idle conversation. We were on our second beers when she abruptly asked if

I danced or not and before I could reply she just grabbed my hand and dragged me onto the dance floor when the DJ put on "I'll be your friend" by Robert Owens. She removed her jacket and beret and as she piled them safely away on a section of the dance floor I watched mesmerized as reams of luxurious hair cascaded down to her waist - in an instant the juvenile looking girl had become a luscious woman in front of my very eyes!

Her bosom, which she had somehow kept hidden all day were even larger than her elder sisters and she smiled a "gotcha" smile as I stood staring in disbelief. And the lady could dance - we spent most of the night on the dance floor or outside talking and by the end of the evening I had decided to defect to Ireland if that was what it would take to win her heart - I was in love like a motherfucker. I would end up seeing Caley almost every day; keeping her company and showing her the sights of Ontario while her sister went off to work or spent time with Ali.

She was fiercely competitive and we sought out pool halls across the province where she embarrassed a host of "professional" players who all got conned by her diminutive teenager routine – she deliberately dressed down to hide her assets and each evening was a new experience – I was simply besotted.

I introduced her to Tantra and pretty soon we were lost within each other and when it came time for her to return home at the end of September she simply refused to go! We carried on dating oblivious to the world until finally her father gave her an ultimatum – either she returned home for Christmas or he would come get her himself, she still had her college to finish.

She booked a ticket for the 23rd of December and we spent the remaining weeks exploring Ontario together. They called the last flight but we refused to let go of each-other, desperately seeking an excuse; anything to hold her back. We stood in the terminal at Pearson Airport, arms locked tightly around each other, listening to our hearts beating in silence.

She felt my need and moved closer, as tears welling in her eyes she whispered "don't let me go." I was lost, confused and madly in love but powerless to act. I still had my course to finish and was not financially stable enough to elope like we'd considered, all we needed was some more time.

There was no doubt in my mind about her as we clicked on every level and she knew more about me in the short period we'd dated than any other woman in my life – she was "the one."

Finally, her waiting sister wrenched us apart and forcibly marched her to the departure gate, my heart breaking as she looked back one last time before a stewardess rushed her into a tunnel. I'd been too upset to even wave.

And that was my last ever view of Caley.

Chapter 3

Bonds of Infinity – Miss. McDonalds

Meeting Kim was all Teng's fault- I had innocently gone to her family restaurant for a meal with Lucy and ended up given her my new number, never expecting her to call, but call she did...

Toronto - late February:

I was by my window, wistfully gazing out at the strolling lovers on Lakeshore Boulevard from my new condo when my phone went off in the kitchen. It was Teng. Teng-Li - The hardest Oriental Tom girl in Ontario or all of Canada as far as I knew. I first met her years back when Dorotka and I were an item. We drove fine German cars - Teng and her crew drove fine Japanese versions.

For months we played a game of cool sleights as we seemed to meet at one after-hour club or another. She had a pretty sidekick who always seemed to accompany her named Emily who was Japanese and they seemed to do everything together. They were obviously of some importance as they were always granted VIP in every single club we saw them at but apart from nods of acknowledgment, we never spoke to each other. But I digress:

Every Sunday Dorotka and I would have a "breakfast date" following a night out clubbing in Mississauga after which we would check into the airport Hilton. She had a passion for their Chef made pancakes, wolfing them down while I watched planes take off and land from Pearson, fiddling with my bearcat scanner. On one such morning we were just about to leave for home and our Sunday ritual of all-day sex and kinkiness when a disheveled looking Teng emerged from the hotel elevator with Emily in Tow.

Their souped up Lexus had given up the ghost (someone had poured sugar in the gas tank while they partied it later emerged), and they needed an "immediate" ride downtown. Despite Dorotka's secret stare of death I graciously agreed and to make matters worse invited them to freshen up at our place when Emily inquired as to the possibility. It seemed her mother was the waiting by the door kind, especially since she had either forgotten or chosen not to call home the previous night. From that day on Teng was but a phone call away, although I never found out what'd happened at the Hilton or who put sugar in their fuel tank.

Dorotka was now gone and out of my life - a painful memory of Channel #5 perfume, nudism and acrobatic sex while Teng and Emily still remained friends with me.

I called her back-

"What's up"?
"Nothing much, just dropped of a friend downtown - where are you?"
"Just chilling at home."
"Got company?"
"Wish I did", I replied as I thumbed through a Cosmopolitan a previous lover had left behind in my kitchen... On page 33 a very blonde Linda Evangelista was semi naked and suddenly I felt life returning to forgotten areas of my anatomy after months of self-imposed bachelorship.

"Hey T, do you know any single women out there looking for a real relationship?"
"Not anyone I'd recommend unless you're really desperate" followed by, "Oh wait I know this chick named Kim but I think she's a virgin..."
A virgin? This would be a new challenge as I'd never ever met any- not even during my year of shame male whoring across Canada.
"A virgin in the T. Dot, what is she – a preacher's daughter or worse?" I laughed.
"No dude – she's quite pretty but very picky and her dad is said to be pretty fierce."

"Gulp..."

I weighed the pros and cons then looked at the Cosmopolitan in my hands - ooh Miss Evangelista! I needed to find a new girlfriend soon, someone I could start my life over with – I could not go back to being a Wolf. Within minutes Teng was in my home and on the phone to Kim -

"Hey Kim do you want to meet my friend with the new BMW?"

She definitely knew her cars because I heard Teng saying to her – "No, not a 3 series, he has the new M5 in Black", followed by a scream of delight from the other end of the phone.

Now I was intrigued; a pretty lady who knew the significance of an M class Bimmer. I couldn't wait to meet her. She was free after 6pm so Teng and I took a cruise to Hamilton, returning to Toronto just after 6.30pm. We parked in a Shopping Centre close to Kim's house and waited.

"I'll bet you fifty bucks you'll like her" said Teng.

"Deal" I foolishly replied.

Five minutes later a virtual clone of the actress Kim Basinger, wearing a simple black turtle neck sweater over jeans stood taking pictures of us in the car. Teng laughed at my expression and explained:

"I forgot to mention – she' a photographer."

The vision of potential delights walked around the car, inspecting it every which way before coming to my window.

"Hey", she smiled - a devious twinkle in her eyes.

"S'up", I replied, trying to be cool.

"Can you open the hood", she demanded?

I opened the hood. As far as I could tell my newly reformed dick was trying to go supersonic in my pants and it could blast off for all I cared; I was smitten. And that is how Kimmy and I met. She jumped in and Teng ever the diplomat invited us to Oakdale mall. Half-way there she "remembered" she had to be home by 9pm so we dropped her off and decided to go watch a movie; technically our first date. We watched Tombstone and then had a late snack at a Taco-Bell, talking about cars and photography until around 2am.

I dropped her off home where we simply shook hands and made a date for the following day - "Any time after 6pm" was good she said.

At half past six the following day we were on a cruise in and around Toronto. By eight pm we were eating at a Red Lobster and then watched "The Empire Strikes Back" together in my condo. She stayed until after midnight, after calling her mom and giving my address and phone number and when I took her home, I finally gave her the kiss I'd been holding back since day one until the windows steamed up in the car.

I drove back home at Mach 5 along Lakeshore Boulevard, racing all the lights in euphoria and the Police couldn't have stopped me if they'd tried that night – I was on fire!

A month or so later we borrowed "Return of the Jedi" from Blockbuster, grabbed a bucket of KFC's finest and had a date on my living room floor. Somewhere between Yoda's transcendence and Obi-Wan telling Luke that Leia was his sister, we magically found ourselves naked and writhing on the bare carpet. At around three am her mother called to politely ask if Kim would be returning home that night - I was single no more.

Kim and I dated for over a year and a half until I stupidly cheated on her in a mad moment of alcoholic weakness after some silly squabble and I rightfully got dumped after I confessed in guilt - I truly cared for her. But she had her morals and I had betrayed her so that was our end. She'll always be special in my heart; she rocked.

Chapter 4

Cassandra - A Futile Resistance

It was a warm Sunday in summer and I decided to treat myself and go out clubbing since I was off work the following week. I washed and waxed my latest toy, a golden BMW E39 and headed for the city centre. The normal routine is to cruise the main strips doing two miles an hour or so with your music blasting – a modern day equivalent of Neanderthal man standing on a cliff top and beating his breasts to show his mighty erection to any interested female parties. Hopefully when you eventually got to the club of your choice at least one female would have recognised your specific idiocy and or ride and gravitate towards you if she liked you, your car or the music you'd played. Hey we were young, stupid and always horny.

Thus, after the requisite cruises up and down Yonge, Bay, Bloor and Adelaide Streets I finally ended up outside of the Limelight club where my mate Mike from England managed security. I parked right outside, to let Mike and his team take turns driving my pride and joy around the block but it was okay – I always got the VIP treatment so they were more than welcome. Mike had broken up with his long-term girlfriend and we moved a few metres from the front door to talk about it. We were deep in conversation when a group of five girls turned the corner and headed straight for us, ostensibly heading for the Limelight. My back was facing the corner and all Mike said was "wow" as his eyes lit up. I turned and did a double take - five ladies had taken over the pavement and were turning heads each and every way.

Mike was tongue-tied for once and simply moved off the pavement and onto the street to let them pass by. I stood rooted to the spot, dazed until they reached me and then parted like water – two passed me on each side but the middle beauty refused to break her stride and came right up to me, pretend shock on her face.

"Are you going to move or what?" she demanded of me.

My heart beating wildly, I dug deep into my psyche and came out with the deepest line I could dredge up:

"Your entire life to date has brought you to this meeting, to this very point and moment in time and you want me to move?" I asked with some seriousness.

Mike almost wet his pants holding in his laughter while two of the beauties who'd stopped to wait for their friend rolled their eyes. But she thought me funny –

"How long have you been practising that line?", she asked with a cute giggle – she had been drinking. I decided to jump right in –

"Since your beauty made me lose my mind" I heard myself respond, as Mike rushed off into the club holding in his sides to prevent himself peeing his pants or worse. The world stood still…

"So, can you get us into the club or not?" She asked me.

"If you tell me your name I'll get you VIP for life and for your number you can drink for free as well" I promised.

"You're on" She replied. She smelt of Wrigley's spearmint gum, with a faint hint of perfume as she grabbed my arm decidedly – I was hooked up.

And that is how I met Cassandra Paige, the disrupter and gate keeper of my soul.

Mike's crew gave us the VIP treatment all evening and once in the club she stuck by my side while her friends mingled and danced. She was a librarian, a Pisces, didn't smoke and "chose to be single because all men are dogs."

"Woof" I agreed, causing her to laugh again. We just seemed to click. Around midnight they decided to check out another club and she invited me to join them, much to the obvious annoyance of her friends – they were meant to be on a girl's night out.

They had parked a few blocks away so she waited with me while they went for their car after I promised to drive her. When they arrived, I unlocked the golden Bimmer parked outside the club and the previously hostile ladies begun seeing me in a new light. Two jumped out of their friend's car to join Cassandra in mine and we headed out to the RPM club where I also knew the bouncers and once again we got the VIP treatment. She was now tired and less talkative than before – she admitted later that she'd felt uncomfortable after seeing my car and had not believed I was single. Nevertheless, she gave me her work number and I promised to call her.

I went back to Mike's club and he warned me to be careful – "there's no way that lady is single" he insisted and I spent the following week concentrating on school and work. About two weeks later I called Mike and he asked about her and I confessed I'd been too busy to call her.

"Give it a shot dude", he advised – "you might get lucky even if she has a man."

Remembering Janice and Glen I decided why not and called the number she'd given me:

A lady with a Jamaican sounding accent answered the telephone –

"Public library, how may I help you"?

"Hello – can I speak to Cassandra please?"

"Which Cassandra?", "This is a public library you know..."

"Well I know she works in that department because she gave me this phone number..."

"What's her last name?" Crap – she had told me but I'd forgotten; it was written on a napkin somewhere in my car...

"I'm sorry I don't know her last name but she's blonde, about 5 feet 6 and very pretty"

"Are you some sort of stalker Sir?", She asked me!

"Look just tell her it's her friend with the gold BMW – we met downtown."

"Hold the line" she said, putting me on hold before I could reply.

I almost hung up in frustration.

"Hey dog, how are you?" said a familiar voice

"Woof" I replied and there was the magical giggle from her again

"Who was that lady, your body guard?" I asked laughing.

"Everyone here is very protective of me" she replied – "That was Mavis - she's a friend of my mother."

Her mom also worked in the library.

"How did you know it was me", I asked.

"It's funny because I talked to my mom about you last week and she asked me at lunch today if you'd called. I just knew it was you."

We ended up making a date for the Saturday. She wanted to do something outside the city so we decided on a day trip to Niagara Falls as our first date and I couldn't wait for the weekend to come.

The following weekend I picked her up from her flat and my heart stopped when she came outside; even dressed casually in a white "Esprit" T shirt, jeans, sandals and minimal make-up she was simply gorgeous. She said a simple "Hi", jumped in and put on her shades.

"Let's go cowboy" she gestured.

"I'm marrying this woman!" I decided on the spot.

So, we drove to the Falls, almost had lunch in a Denny's restaurant (she later confessed if I'd eaten the slimy and suspicious soup we got served that would have been the end of "us"), did the touristy bit and had dinner in a proper restaurant before heading back home in the evening. We talked about simply everything and on the way back I asked her bluntly if she would "consider being my new girlfriend."

She thought for a minute and then asked me if I'd seen "When Harry met Sally" and Meg Ryan's character in the movie.

I said "Yes."

"Well that's what you're going to get if we date – I'm very high maintenance" she confessed.

"In that case I think I'll have what you ordered", I responded and she cracked up.

I drove her home and went over to open the door for her like a gentleman, and as she got out she just grabbed me and let me have it. We must have kissed for an hour or so before we realised half the windows in the flats above were filled with spectators - I was single no more. Despite sleeping over in her flat sometimes we waited for close to three months before "doing it" to prove I was not a dog who was only interested in her body.

Of course, we were both mad with lust by then which made the experience even more magical and meaningful. Everyone agreed we were "The Perfect Couple" and we lasted over three incredible years, experiencing adventures and situations bordering on the stuff of movies. We would travel the USA from coast to coast, almost get shot by a nervous Policewoman in Montreal, watch an outstanding Sunset kiss the far-off shores of Cuba from a beach in Key-West, Florida and bump into celebrities on Rodeo-Drive in Beverly-Hills. We've toured both Disney-Land and Disney-World parks, argued while speeding through Death Valley, spent romantic weekends in Newark and Manhattan, made crazy love on USA A1-A in a moving vehicle and wrecked hotel beds across Canada in our passions. She stuck by me through thick and thin and we've shed tears of pleasure, pain, relief and the joys of Tantra together - she was all woman.

There's still the outstanding question of Vancouver as a suitable place to raise a new family and I still wouldn't change anything except maybe eloping with and marrying her the very first week I met her, to prevent eventualities which would see us torn-apart some years down the line.

Just like with Caley - we never officially "broke up" and I was working on getting her over to finally join me England when she sadly lost both her amazing parents and our worlds fell apart.

I once made a promise in Montreal, many years ago, to a woman I truly and deeply loved: Eternity is forever, Time is but a Dream and "Hay, it could still happen."

Chapter 5

Bayswater Rules

The plane landed at Heathrow airport exactly on time and I waited patiently for the other passengers to disembark before reaching up into the overhead compartment for my stuff. As I headed for the exit I met a stewardess coming towards me, checking to make sure no one had forgotten something behind. I stood aside to let her pass and my heart beat faster as she smiled at me. Her name tag read Samantha - I'd been scoping her throughout the flight and almost choked when she addressed me directly:

"So, did he win"? She asked me with a mischievous smile on her face.

"Sorry?",

I managed to blurt out; being so close to her in the confines of the narrow walkway was triggering hormones in my nether regions.

"Larry", she replied, nodding at my laptop bag, firmly clamped under my armpit –

"I noticed you spent most of the flight playing", she explained.

"Oh Larry", I bumbled…

"Well we came close but no, story of my life", I managed to blurt out. She smiled again, and then quickly seemed to come to a decision.

"Are you staying long in London then"?

"Five years, maybe longer if my life improves."

She laughed, and then blushing slightly came to the point –

"Sunday evening Bar Rhumba in Piccadilly",

"Tell them Martin sent you"

"Martin?"

"Yes, Martin", she whispered in my ears "just like in Larry."

She held onto my elbow and guided me to the door, winking at the other stewardesses at the door before adding - "We'll all be there, ask any party girls you see on Sunday night where bar Rhumba is."

I shook my head in wonder - it seemed London was not going to be as lonely as I'd feared – I'd literally just gotten off the plane from Canada and I already had a date! I checked into my hotel with a giddy mixture of elation and couldn't wait until the Sunday. I found Bar Rhumba as advertised and actually managed to skip the line-up with the "Martin sent me" phrase – it turned out Martin was the head of security.

I had a wonderful evening with Samantha, Rebecca and Denise, the stewardesses from my flight made a dinner date with Samantha for the following weekend: they already had pre-arranged plans for their two days in London so they left the club early. I decided to finish my drink and head back to my hotel and maybe catch up on my sleep as I was still a little jet-lagged and as I headed up the stairs for the exit a pretty young lady was coming downstairs and I just stopped half-way up the staircase, stunned. I smiled and she smiled back and as she reached me I simply took her hand –

"Wow but you're gorgeous" – "tell me you're single and we can get married today, my search is over!"

She shook her head and laughing replied –

"Yes, I am single but I think I'll need a strong drink before I get married", she deadpanned.

We headed back downstairs into the club, holding hands - I had just met Eva: a visiting beauty from the Czech Republic. We went to the bar and after a few drinks ended up on the dance floor for a while, before deciding to go walking in the west-end. We would end up sitting by the fountains in Trafalgar Square and just talking until dawn, at which point we took a taxi to Battersea where she was staying with some friends for the summer.

We made plans to meet again the next day at Bar Salsa, a Cuban club she knew close to Leicester Square. She was already there when I showed up and we had a fun night of Tango dancing and Tequila, followed by a visit to a Nando's restaurant. It's like the Keg in Toronto except they serve grilled chicken with lots of pepper but more importantly, you can get beer with your food and I became a fan of San Miguel beer. We then embarked on a "Welcome to London" ritual of stopping at every single pub we came across in the West-end for a single drink and by the time we left Carnaby street I was speaking Latin.

Later that evening she asked to see where I lived and so we took the tube to Bayswater and my hotel, where she ordered me to take my shirt off so she could give me a massage - she did not beat about the bush. I returned the favor after I sobered up and we ended up dating for a few months until she abruptly left for Germany with an older and richer guy she bumped into in my hotel lobby - not even tantric sex was going to disrupt her chance for a better life.

I did not cry, this was London after all and the rules were different - in Bayswater, money talks.

Chapter 6

The Angel of Corvallis – Tanith's Tale

It was just one date, done more out of curiosity than anything else. Granted he was funny and good looking in a certain way - the truth was she was from a small town in Oregon and a little terrified of London. Her first week had been spent within the environs of her hotel and though he'd smiled at her during breakfast – she had pretended not to notice. On the third day of her second week in London they'd bumped into each other in the hotel lobby and he'd finally introduced himself. He smelt very nice and she noticed he had amazingly white teeth. The next day he sat at the table next to hers during breakfast and they had chit-chatted politely.

When he invited her into the city center on the weekend she eagerly agreed - visiting Piccadilly Circus was high on her agenda but the prospect of going there alone terrified her. The date was therefore made - Tanith was about to meet the world.

They waked all the way into Central London along Bayswater road which had then turned into the famous Oxford Street after they went pass the Marble Arch. With thousands of tourists bustling around them and speaking a multitude of languages and the fascinating array of gigantic luxury stores and new vistas on every street corner she soon lost all track of time. And her "date" seemed to have answers to every question she asked and somewhere along the route she realized she'd been gripping tightly onto his arm like a jealous lover for the past couple of miles.

He didn't seem to mind and before long they were telling each other their life's stories with explicit details. She told him about her break-up with her high-school sweetheart and only lover (he teased her when she admitted they had only "really done it a few times" as she had wanted to wait until after marriage but had given in from fear of losing him, "the jerk" she added.)

She playfully punched her escort as she blushingly admitted doing it "actually, okay maybe six times."

"You're basically still a virgin", he teased

"No, I'm not - how many times have you done it then?", she asked

"You mean this year or all my life he responded?"

"This year?", she asked uncertainly.

"Let's see - January, February, what month is this, October? – Oh, I'd say maybe roughly eighty times or so this year."

She was shocked and he laughed at the expression on her face as he said it.

"My goodness - I'm walking around with a male slut!"

"That's nothing - I know guys who have sex like three or more times each day"

"No way – that's too much" she challenged -

"This is London baby - everyone's in love with someone..."

"Who are you in love with then?", She asked.

"No one at the moment, my ex-girlfriend took off for Germany with some rich old guy she met at the hotel..."

"I'm sorry to hear that" -

"Well - life goes on..."

"That's true - when I found out my ex was cheating on me I thought my life was over"- "It's why I came to London, to forget him."

He hugged her closer and for a moment she was tempted to kiss him but caught a hold of herself "what am I doing?" she asked herself. They walked on in silence for a while, just holding hands, sharing a new bond – that of betrayed lovers among their own kin.

Eventually they stopped at an Ed's Diner to eat and it was only then that she realized she'd spent over six hours with a complete stranger and she didn't want the day to end.

She agreed to his offer of alcohol with their meal and halfway through their meal had switched seats to sit next to him. After their meal they walked through Piccadilly, then passed through Leicester square where they danced with some street musicians and shared some ice cream. After feeding pigeons around Trafalgar square they walked to Buckingham Palace and from there went past Victoria coach station and wandered around until they arrived in Knightsbridge.

As they turned a corner he asked her to close her eyes and yelled "Surprise" and right in front of them was the famous Harrods store. They went inside, where he bought her some souvenir handkerchiefs. From there they walked past the Museum of Natural History, through Holland park Gardens and finally arrived in Notting-Hill where they stopped at the Sun in Splendor Pub for dinner and a few pints.

She was tired but elated - she had seen and done more in one day than she had dreamed possible. They agreed to do some more sight-seeing together and hugged each other goodnight in the hotel lobby. The next day they went on a bus ride through London. Bus #83 to Pimlico meanders from south of the river Thames through central London, and then proceeds west along the Bayswater road through Notting-Hill, Kensington and Hammersmith, before finally stopping on the boarders of Fulham. It's was the perfect way to fully discover London as they rode it all the way into London and then back to the end of the route, laughing and giggling like two teenagers.

They finally exited at Fulham and then walked back through Chelsea, High Street

Kensington and By 9pm when they finally left to walk back to their hotel in Bayswater she had decided she loved him.

Just like that.

When they arrived in the lobby he politely said goodnight and as he went to hug her she kissed him on the cheek and whispered "see you at breakfast." They had breakfast together the next morning and took a walk down to the Portobello Road market, holding hands – something had definitely changed between them and they could both sense it. Portobello road had everything from Antiques, Art from upcoming Artists, New and old clothes, books and electronics – it was like being in an Aladdin's cave of wonders to her and the time seemed to fly.

When they finally got tot the top of the market she realized they had spent almost four hours in the market talking to the myriad of sellers, shoppers and street performers. That night they watched a concert together in Hyde Park, and there under the stars, they kissed for the first time, surrounded by other young lovers. And that night, in his hotel room, Tanith made sweet love for the seventh time to a man who made pleasing her his main priority.
It was simply magical.

Chapter 7

Olga - A Russian Love Affair
"Till the Season's end ,
and every creature has its turn in the sun,
Time will remain endless."

I first met Olga in the spring, a visiting Russian beauty who had been snapped up as a cash-in hand receptionist by the astute owners of an internet cafe I serviced weekly. It was located in Bayswater, in a posh neighborhood close to Notting-Hill, an area frequented by rich Arabs, bored models and movie stars, and close to the residences of the oligarchs and assorted monied men who lived nearby in Chelsea and South Kensington. Her presence of course increased the Internet Café's customer base as word soon spread and people came from near and far to use the then novel "Internet" facility in the hope of maybe getting lucky; this was London after all and most Eastern Europeans girls were known to be quite "friendly" if albeit a bit naive or so the common misconceptions went.

They never stood a chance. With survival instincts honed by growing up beautiful in Eastern Europe, in addition to an Economics degree hidden beneath her "clueless" smile, she wove her magic with a ready laugh, leaving behind her a host of enthralled, dejected and broken-hearted aspirants. My salvation was the fact that I had an attractive Czech girlfriend when Olga and I first met (Eva), and therefore I was not overly overwhelmed by her beauty as I would otherwise have been. This turned out to be a blessing in disguise as we simply became platonic friends; slowly getting to know each other during my service calls and pretty soon a year had gone by during which time my previous girl-friend and I had split-up.

The Christmas season with its degree of loneliness for those far from home and the recently separated, worked in our favor and so Olga and I drifted closer together, two lost souls hanging out for simple companionship and pretty soon I was giving her rides home from work in my second-hand Volvo as a friend. The magic eventually happened one night when she kissed me out of the blue: of all the guys she knew I was the "only one not trying desperately to get into her pants" and suddenly I had found myself a new girlfriend. And so, it came to pass as these things naturally do, we became pregnant after a wonderful year of bliss and adventures which included her almost getting run-over by an infatuated National-Express coach driver outside of Victoria station, and my blindly following her through a live Ministry of Defense minefield while out on a "romantic walk" during a visit to Surrey. I would have died for Olga back then and years later, I almost would.

We were the ideal couple, with two sons and living in marital bliss until her jealous elder sister who was stuck back home and had already ditched husband number one, started manipulating Olga to leave me. She could not very well leave husband number two and escape to Europe while her younger sister celebrated years of bliss and harmony with me in London. The minute poor Olga caved in to her threats and finally left me, the evil sister dumped husband number two and the father of her children and emigrated for greener pastures. By time Olga saw the light it was too late: Dorotka had thought me one valuable lesson - once betrayed there's

never going back: I would eventually heal
and seek love again.

Chapter 8

ODE TO LIBERTY
(A Dedication to Olga)

Flee, begone, vanish from my sight,
Oh, ye feeble princess of Cythera
Thou, lofty muse of Liberty,
Where art thou, bane of kings, come nearer!
A garland of flowers from me wrench,
Smash down with hands the coddled lyre…
I sing of Freedom's victorious fire
Chastised vice enthroned on royal bench.

Reveal to me the noble path
Of the self-aggrandized Gaul
In whom amidst famed catastrophe
Thou inspired hymns audacious
Nurslings of frivolous Destiny,
Tyrants of the world! Tremble!
And ye, take heart and pay attention,
Rise up, trampled slaves!

Alas! Wherever I cast (my) gaze
Everywhere scourges, everywhere irons,
The laws' destructive mockery,
Serfdom's helpless tears;
Everywhere lawless sovereignty
The heavy fog of prejudice
Has confirmed – slavery's dreaded Genius
And Glory's baneful intensity.

There only upon the royal head
The nation's quilt has not come to lie
Where potent with sacred Liberty
Is powerful laws' association
Where to all is offered their firm shield
Where, grasped by steadfast hands
Rise up protecting citizens, of equal heads
Their sword glissades without choice

To attack the breach from on high
With righteous force;
Where honesty is their hand
By either eager greed or fear.
Monarchs! To your crown and throne
The law delivers – and not nature;
Ye stand superior above the nation,
Higher still than ye infinite Law.

And woe, misery to the family
Where it hot-headedly slumbers,
Where for nations or for kings
It is feasible to override the laws!
Thee I assemble you all to witness,
Oh, martyr of infamous fallacies,
Who for an ancestry in rebellious storms
Lay down his sovereign head.

Up steps Louis to his death
In full view of voiceless progeny,
Without his crown he bowed his head
To the bloody scaffold of Mutiny.
Mute the Law –mute the nation,

There swings the unlawful axe…
And lo – a corrupted purple
Lies like all shackled Gaul.

Autocratic Miscreant!
Thee, thy throne I detest,
Descent means thy children's death
With savage delight I see.
Nations perceive upon thy brow
The sign of execration,
Thou [art] the horror of the world, a
disgrace of nature,
A rebuke to God on earth.

When on the murky Neva
The star of midnight shone
And the worry-free head
Subdued sleep weighs down
The thoughtful singer gazes
Upon the threatened sleeping midst the
haze
Abandoned monument of the tyrant,
The palace deserted to oblivion –

Echoes of terror, Cleo's voice erupts
Behind fortresses a summons tolling
Caligula's last hour beckons us
Before he sees a vivid fate unrolling,
He sees, in ribbons and in stars
By poison and with wine befuddled,
The secretive assassins huddled
Insolent faces over fear filled hearts.

And silence visits the disloyal watchman,
To drop the drawbridge at midnight season,
In secret gloom the gate unbarred
By hired hands of mercenary treason.
Oh, shame, Oh, horror lately found!
The Janissaries thrust in, appalling
Like beasts, irreverent blows befalling…
Till butchered lies the miscreant crowned.

Henceforth, oh, kings learn, and know this true:
That neither flattery nor halters
Make sturdy barricades for you,
Neither prison walls, nor holy altars.
Be ye first to bow your head down
Beneath the canopy of Law eternal.
The people joyous, their freedom vernal
Will forever save the nation's crown.

– Alexander Pushkin

(Translation by **M.A. DuVernet**)

Chapter 9

London Calling - A Sunday Story

I watch her drink Lipton's iced tea on the central line; a pretty blonde with green nail polish wearing strawberry colored slippers. She has piercing green eyes, almost animal like in their intensity and she is sat directly opposite me - a look of "Je ne care pas what you think" on her face as she has her breakfast; two fresh chocolate croissants in a "Prêt a Manger" bag.

She eats the croissants in exactly seven and a half bites; all pretense of ladylike behavior gone as primal hunger beckons – she seems famished. She pauses on her third bite – the train announcer apologizing to Chancery Lane passengers – it seems the station is closed hence the tube would not be stopping there. A slight shrug; then a quick glance around at the other inhabitants of the carriage and then seemingly unimpressed, she re-attacks the croissants with renewed gusto.

"The next station is Holborn, please change here for the Piccadilly line", the voice of the tube lady pipes.
Mild hesitation to take in the new information, a quick lick of her lips and then bites four and five follow in quick succession. She munches quickly, mouth closed, unconsciously

brushing back her hair with her left hand as she chews. She pauses mid bite, to gaze at the peeling nail polish on her index finger and then remembering the task in hand, polishes of the last bit of pastry with an urgent fury. She looks at her empty hand, seemingly unable to believe the croissants are finished, and then sighs in resignation. She proceeds to put the empty pastry wrapper into her handbag with a sense of loss, then spotting her leftover bottle of Lipton's Iced tea, takes two quick quaffs in ecstasy; emptying it.

She sighs again and I cannot help wondering what she'd be like in bed – all sighs and contentment I imagine. She rummages through her bag, searching then finally gives up with another sigh.
She gets off the tube at Oxford Circus, glancing at me and my pad as I write this.

Our eyes meet as the doors close. Was that a knowing smile?

The tube departs.

Chapter 10

The Art of being "Interesting"

Whenever I lost a girlfriend I would always think back to my first love and reminisce of a simpler time when love was pure and innocent…

An uneventful summer had passed and I was getting ready to depart secondary school for University and its promises of female potential. Meanwhile I still hung around the school library in my spare time as it was the only place I could freely use a computer in peace and one day "she" literally walked into my life. It was a sunny Friday afternoon and there were exactly four people in the library, myself included. The librarian was not at his desk, and the other two library users were up on the second floor – two teenage girls whispering and giggling in equal measure across the empty aisles.

I was sitting close to the door, on the top stair leading into the library when she hesitantly got out of the Taxi. All I could see was that she had to be the bombshell of the century; a veritable Marilyn Monroe clone who was obviously lost – she had no business being on campus with the body and face she had. She gave me a nervous smile to which I replied with a wide-eyed nod as she walked past me to the reception desk. She was wearing a form fitting floral dress in light green plastered with daffodils over short black stilettos and a mesmerising pair of leggings topped off with a black handbag and looked ravishing. After patiently waiting for some five minutes at the desk she looked around, caught me staring and walked back to me.

"Hello, can you tell me how to get to the Principal's office please?" she asked.

My heart beating wildly, I simply nodded, stood up and walked outside as she followed me in silence. Half-way across the quad I picked up the nerve to introduce myself and found out she was a relief teacher, that her name was Deborah and she had just flown in from England the day before. She was from Canvey Island. Her meeting with the head teacher lasted an hour or so and when she came out I was still waiting in a chair outside of the office, engrossed in my John Fowles novel.

"The Aristos!" she exclaimed in obvious delight. I simply shrugged –

"I love making", I started to quote and she replied;

"I love doing..."

We both laughed and she looked at me with some interest - I then heard myself confess,

"I also like the works of Dostoevsky, Pushkin

and Camus."

She cocked her head in a manner I was to find out was a trait of hers and half-smiling asked if I could do her another favour.

"It depends", I blurted out.

The teasing smile again and then -

"Can you show me to the staff room and where I can make some photo copies?"

My courage returning, I answered cheekily –

"If you agree to be my friend I'll do anything you want."

"Deal, lead the way then."

I simply nodded, turned around and led the way – I could feel her gaze on my butt as I walked because my collar got hot. After escorting her around the main office I shyly invited her out to a movie that night and I was pleasantly surprised when she agreed - she seemed to find me "interesting", much to the consternation of the entire campus.

My only handicap in reality was the fact I still lived at home and therefore had a curfew. It was time to confront "The Terminator", i.e. my father as the movie ended very late and way past my curfew. The weekend was going to be a genuine disrupter – I was going to butt heads with the twin forces of potential homelessness and of being the laughing stock of the entire student body if she stood me up but I wasn't going to miss this date for anyone or anything.

My parents had gone to visit friends in the country-side and timing things perfectly; I called the friend some twenty minutes before they got there.

"Can you tell my parents I'll be staying over at my mate Joe's tonight", I lied – I need to help him finish up some homework..."

"No problem", came the response - I was free.

We met as agreed in the lobby of the cinema, at the time the only cinema in Blantyre and being a Friday, half of the clients were from my school and most people were wondering who the latest heartthrob was. I almost chickened out from nerves.

She looked ravishing and was dressed to kill and sensing my nervousness walked up to me and kissed me on the cheek before giving me a playful punch and whispering to me -

"If the movie sucks we can leave early..."

Was that innuendo? I warmed up inside and suddenly felt like a giant. Foregoing all the latest releases, she chose "Desperately

Seeking Susan", starring Madonna.

We watched the movie surrounded by astounded faces from our school and despite dying to hold her hand I did not make a move. After the movie ended she surprised me by offering to treat me to dinner in her hotel's restaurant as it was open till late. "Great", I thought to myself.

Dinner saw her open up and we talked about everything under the sun while drinking unhealthy amounts of beer until the hotel's restaurant closed for the night, at which point we found ourselves a quit place in the lobby to continue our conversation. We conversed almost non-stop, laughing and joking together like old friends in the hotel lobby until dawn broke. I realized I had not been tongue-tied once the entire evening and I walked on air all the way home. We astounded the entire school population when we began dating – she thought I was "different and quite interesting..." and I would go on to lose my virginity with her.

"Interesting" – whenever I heard the expression I thought back to my first love Deborah and I suddenly felt sad about the whore I had become. Being "interesting" could get one in trouble on the female front.

Lots of trouble.

Chapter 11

Joie de Vivre – Lessons from France

It happened at the Sainsbury's at the top of Harrow Road, as one went up from Notting-hill Gate. I'd gone looking for my daily ration of protein from the hot food counter and being late, decided to cut through the baby products section. The noon crowd were afoot; hungry office types who bought more than they could eat just to spite the lucky ones who went in early during "reduction hour" after six pm, to pick up bargains for pennies.

A lunchtime sandwich costing three pounds would be reduced to fifteen pence at dusk, making for some very angry office types who happened on the store on their way home from work. This state of affairs had now resulted in some office types deliberately clearing out the deli section during lunch, in an effort to prevent any leftovers from being reduced: the logic was ludicrous but then such is human nature.

Thus, on my quest to grab myself a meal I went through the baby section, hoping to bypass the mid-afternoon crowd and turning a corner quickly, I collided with one of the most gorgeous creatures on the planet in my haste. It was a mixture of pain, excitement, embarrassment and curiosity all rolled into one. She dropped the bottle of herbal essences shampoo she'd been holding and I caught it mid fall, somehow also managing to grab her arm to prevent her falling. We gazed into each other's eyes and as she apologized I went numb. Holding out the shampoo to her I heard myself blurt out-

"My goodness, you cannot possibly be this good looking…"

She took a while to ingest my words and then blushing slightly simply replied

"Thank you…"

It seemed like the world stood still - I could hear her breathing and smell minute details - she smelt of cinnamon chewing gum, hair of fructose essentials (of course) and a slight hint of perfume; possibly hand cream with traces of jasmine. Her perfectly manicured nails were covered with clear varnish -

I took all this in within seconds.

"You're staring" she said and smiled, slightly blushing. I was still holding her shampoo like a hostage - I transferred it to my left hand as I extended the right -

'Hi, I'm Jordan'

Instinctively she responded, holding out her hand before she could think –

"Simone'." She had an accent.

She smiled and I smiled back gazing into her eyes. For a second, we looked into each other's souls then came to a mutual decision - we shopped together, and then walked together to the checkout, and proceeded to the car park in joyful silence: things were looking up.

"Are you driving I asked?"

"No, I live not far, at the end of the road."

I brush back a strand of hair from across her face and ask her if she'll have lunch with me? She hesitates slightly and then comes to a decision-

"Only if you let me cook for us"

"Fine" I reply, "but only if I can help".

"Do you cook?" she asks and I finally place the accent - she is French!

"Lady you have no clue", I respond, followed by 'I cannot believe how beautiful you are'

She blushes slightly-

"Please stop saying that…"

"Okay. Do you have a boyfriend?"

"No"

"Can I be your boyfriend then, please?"

"I don't know, maybe - if you want?"

It was that simple.

It is really true – the prettier the lady the lonelier she usually turns out to be.

Thinking back to Lucy, I take a gamble and tell her to pucker up.

She does so and in the car-park surrounded by the whole world it seems, I kissed her like it was the end of the world.

Simone' was in London for a year and worked part-time at a posh sandwich shop in the West-End while attending a business course for an economics degree. She was from a small town near Nice and had broken up with her long-term boyfriend before coming over to London. We would date for a year before she went back home and we left things unplanned as she had to finish her course back in France - we agreed to date others in the meantime. She ended up taking an internship in Argentina and is currently dating a local doctor whom "she cannot stand" but plans to return to London sometime in the future. She still calls me now and then when she's lonely and yes, we've had phone sex as "we never really broke up", as she often reminds me.

My wife has no problem with my still talking to any of my exes "as long as they're a continent away and it's just phone sex" which she thinks is "silly but funny." I don't think I deserve my wife and each time I tell her she replies with "true love will withstand anything." I think she pities me somehow for all the whoring I've done when she talks of "Love conquering all." I am still adrift...

Chapter 12

Simone' – Tall Tales & Tequila

"Tell me a story", she demanded after dinner, a sultry edge to her voice and a glint in her eyes. She was bored and whenever she got bored she'd pick a fight which usually ended in her giving me the silent treatment until I figured out what was wrong. I put it down to a quirk of being French and the trick was to get her interested in something, or better yet laughing, in which case I was guaranteed to get lucky. She was strange like that.

I thought long and hard and then cleared my throat as she put her head in my lap and gazed at me in rapt attention. I began –

"So, Freddy Mercury (She loves the music of Queen), had a pet Penguin named Saul..."

"He had bought a fancy mansion unseen in the Hollywood Hills and going in to inspect it, he found a penguin just lolling on a settee smoking a Cohiba from Cuba..." (Simone' giggles – "looking good, keep going I think")

"So, you're the new boss", the Penguin remarked, not looking too impressed.

"I must be dreaming or high, thought Mr. Mercury."

"And why would you think that?" the penguin asked.

"You can read my mind?" He asked incredulously.

"Of course – why do you think we moved far away from humans? Because we don't trust you and every Penguin is a telepath pal."

"No way"

"Yes way."

"And you can all talk?"

"Like, Duh!"

"Wow."

"You can say that again - If you ask me we should be running this planet like we used to."

"Penguins used to run the planet?", asked Freddy

"Of course. Long before humans came here we ruled my friend!"

"What are you trying to say?"

"I'm not saying anything, replied the Penguin, looking furtively around"

"What is furtively?", Simone' interrupted. I explained, then carried on with the story-

"I've said too much as it is", said Saul...

"You my friend are an Alien though."

"What? What do you mean," Freddy spluttered...?

"The Penguin looked away, looking in silhouette like a young Sherlock Holmes with his pipe...."

Simone' stirred in my lap, with her eyes now half closed - debating whether to carry on with my now obviously boring story or proceed directly to something else I hoped. She suddenly stood up, yawned and stretched, shaking her head as she caught me staring at her pretty bottom.

"Chien", she said with a half-smile, then bent down to quickly kiss me -

 "I'm getting a beer – you want one?"

Beer was good.

In fact, it was excellent as I needed help - I had no idea where my story was headed...

This was great as getting a beer meant she really wanted to listen to my story. Now I really had to bore her before the beer took over or we would spend all night arguing the logic to my story and debating the plausibility of certain parts. She was just like that. She returned with the beers and sat opposite me on one end of the Sofa, a stockinged leg under each of my arms as I sat similarly facing her.

She smoothed her skirt after giving me a brief glimpse of her lovely regions; she never wore underwear when we were alone at home – the future looked bright.

"Bud or Corona?" she offered, holding both beers up.

"You choose first I responded". She looked lost; beer wasn't her strong suit.

"How about we share sips?", I suggested. She brightened up and opened the Corona, passing it to me before opening the Bud.

We toasted each other, took a sip each and swapped beers, laughing at our silly ritual. She cocked her head and smiling sweetly asked me to continue my story, sitting up rapt with attention and looking ravishing. I took a long swig of the Budweiser and offered it back to her and after taking a sip she put it on the floor, rather than passing it over - it was story time: now I had to deliver...

"The Penguin said his name was Saul and that he had a twin brother named Paul who lived in the San-Diego zoo but could leave anytime he wanted to visit his brother. He chose to stay at the zoo, in order to know what was happening in the Penguin Kingdom in their absence- apparently, they were Penguin royalty and could be called back home any day…" Simone' interrupted me –

"What is Saul doing in LA, and how are they getting news from Antarctica if ze brother is in ze zoo?", she questioned in her French accent

"The seals and penguins get all the latest news from the dolphins, who have access to the ocean at SeaWorld", I explained.

"No, they don't" she argued, "they stay in ze tank at SeaWorld - I visit as a child."

"Yes" I replied thinking fast, "They live in SeaWorld but their enclosure is built within the sea, so they get to talk to the fish and sometime get visits from free dolphins when humans are not around…"

I was starting to sweat…

"Hmm – okay continue, but why is he in LA?"

"Well the millionaire who owned Saul was actually Paul's human servant" I replied

"How come?"

"Well you see dolphins can time travel and they sometimes give helpful information to penguins to pass on to friendly humans…"

Her frown deepened –

"You know, stuff like winning lottery numbers and such…"

"Oh, I see, that's super; she was now nodding her head. They get a human to buy ze house and live secretly as ze pets, that's smart"

"Exactly" I added enthusiastically – If I kept it up she would take up the story herself – she had a very vivid imagination.

"So, but why LA?" she insisted

"Well, all the animal royalty lives in California, because all the rich people are there so they know they will be safe…"

"Safe from who?"

"Well most animals don't really trust humans, as Saul was telling Freddy…"

"Oh Freddy – I love Freddy"

"I know sweetie, that's why he's in the story"

"Thank you. I love you too you know?"

"I know – I still can't believe how beautiful…"

"Mon Dieu" – "You want to make love to me all ze time non?", "is why you always tell me I'm so beautiful" she complained.

"Mais it's true Cherie."

"Non. Not true - I go to Paris to model and they say to me to lose weight and also, I am too tall, merde!" she swore.

"No way "

"Yes way! That's why I come to London to study instead; anyway, you want to make love now?"

Phew, I was off the hook.

I pulled her closer...

Chapter 13

An Essex Angel – Rachel

We met on a train from Leicester to Nottingham one cold Friday morning. She was an attractive blonde and had a large pencil case filled with assorted artists' stencils, pens and pencils open next to her on the table. She was sat on a table seat, next to the window - wearing a black 'North-Face' jacket with her bags scattered next to her in the aisle seats and propping up a large drawing pad; all defiantly arranged on the seat and silently screaming out – 'No you may not sit next to me!'

Beneath her oversized jacket she had on a monogrammed hoodie emblazoned with the Lacoste Crocodile, over a faded pair of jeans completed by a pair of black Dr. Martin's boots in a size 5 or 6. I pay attention to details like that when it comes to the ladies. I had been on a search for a seat with a power socket and seeing the empty seat opposite her asked her if I could sit? I sat anyway as she was nodding her guarded permission.

She looked stunning.

We gave each other "the look" and psyches' locked, pretended to ignore each other for the hour-long trip while surreptitiously taking each other's photos. She initiated it by taking a selfie first and then pretending to pose for another, she took my photo. I had heard of this trick from a female co-worker and so I smiled directly at her as she took the photo and perturbed at being caught out, she pretended to look out the carriage window, blushing slightly. I had been right.

I got her back in the same way and shaking her head slightly gave a half smile as if saying "fair's fair". She registered disappointment as I took out my Kindle tablet and set it up for a movie and her phone chirped just as I put on my headphones, surreptitiously watching her as she spent some fifteen minutes furiously exchanging text messages on her iPhone with someone – it seemed pretty serious.

It looked final when she finally finished, glaring in anger at her phone with flashing green eyes and a determined set to her jaw.

Wow I thought to myself.

She finally stopped glaring at her phone to look up as I took out my own iPhone, booked my connecting train and laid it pointedly on the table next to her pencil case. She'd regained her composure and put hers down too, her phone almost kissing mine as we both turned to the views of the countryside sweeping past. Her eyes gradually softened and I debated the logic of trying to engage her in conversation as she'd looked furious. Twice our eyes met directly, almost questioning - who was going to speak first?

The silence was almost deafening.

She rummaged in her bag arranging her pencils and stuff as I pretended to watch my movie, all the time gazing at the curve of her neck, her full lips and unkempt blonde her.

It was as if she woke up, threw some clothes on and headed straight for the station: this is me in the raw, no makeup and no apologies, take it or leave it - this is all you get and I don't give a damn what you think. She had blue painted nails and her baggy sweatshirt could not hide the fact she was blessed with some very ample assets. She looked luscious and immensely edible.

She gazed up as I had that thought and gave a coy smile as she caught me staring - perhaps she was psychic. She sent off a final short text and turned her phone off and then putting on a set of headphones, settled herself in her seat. She looked straight into my eyes, then closed hers - "dream of me" if you will, she seemed to telegraph.

I gazed wistfully as her face went through a variety of moods with the music she was listening to, then gazed intently at her fingers - no signs of recent rings. It was Carpe' Diem time because I was attracted to her and she seemed friendly enough to warrant a try – I had been divorced and steadfastly single for some five and had not been attracted to a single woman until now I realized with a shock.

I decided to write her a love letter right there on the train and pass it to her on my iPhone. I was going for broke and would get off at the next station if my reading of the situation was just fantasy and she got angry or upset.

"Dearest pretty stranger sitting opposite me – Hello, I'm Jordan and no I'm not a creep.

I simply think you're amazing and would like to thank you for allowing me to bask in the awesomeness of your exquisite presence. I'm headed for Nottingham and from there catch a connecting train to my final destination - I may never see you again in my life but if there's a possibility of buying you a drink before we say goodbye I'd like to take it.

We're after all alone together at this moment in time and I think you're simply divine and someone I would love to remember as having gazed upon..." I wondered if I was being too effusive but that was how I felt – beauty like hers warranted desperate measures and she probably knew my words were true anyway...

Was she scarier than "my lion" from way back? Definitely not.

Her eyes were still shut as I turned my phone around and slowly placed it in front of her. It was uncanny - She immediately opened her eyes as I did so, simply picked up my phone and begun to read. I closed my eyes, waiting, my heart pounding and my palms starting to sweat....

An eternity passed, she must be a slow reader I was thinking and then a definitive and angelic voice softly called out my name - 'Jordan!'

I opened one eye to find her holding my phone out to me, a smile on her face as she slowly shook her head at my audacity.

I read her response with alacrity....

"What took you so long, asshole - I've been dying to speak to you. Yes, I'd love a drink, Rachel x"

She had enclosed a selfie of herself smiling as well.

All I could think of was "good looking and she swears too." And that is how I finally met "the one".

Some fifteen years after losing my virginity, multiple failed relationships, a year of debauchery and then marriage followed years later by a painful divorce which led to five years abstaining from any kind of relationship or physical contact - she finally showed up out of the blue. Not in a rave, festival or even a pub – we met on a train!

And the most bewildering fact of all - she originally hails from Essex, from a town "very close" to Canvey Island and had studied in Montreal for five years around the time I was self-destructing after my "Dorotka season" in Canada. She had also visited Toronto a few times but never liked "the vibe", and we might actually have crossed paths as she'd visited some of the clubs I used to frequent.

But there is a final kicker and the most mind-boggling of coincidences: She is also a teacher like my first love – She teaches Art History and is exactly six years younger than myself. She would end up proposing to me as I had become afraid of being rejected again, however marrying her was a no brainer.

One day while out on a drive a few months after we started dating, I took her hand and starting singing "Good King Wenceslas" for no apparent reason; it wasn't even Christmas. She looked at me strangely and explained later, that her dad used to do the exact same thing and sing the exact same song to her when she was a child and they went out for a drive. It seems the Universe does have a sense of humor. I rest my case.

Chapter 14

Love's Lessons- A Global Education

(Interviewed with Rachel)

What exactly is "true love" and how do you go about it?

1.   Is "True Love" even possible in a world of on-line dating, casual sex, easy access to porn and the consumerism of the marriage act?

I had been conflicted because I always equated sex with Love as a young Catholic - I could not think of anything more sacred than sharing one's body with another; that is until I had my heart broken and I lost my way. I eventually learned through Tantra, that one can divorce one's feelings from the Sex act and still maintain clarity. For example - I still Love Lucy deeply, despite the fact we've never had sex, and still have love in my heart for my exe's Caley, Kim and Cassandra despite our years apart and their subsequent marriages.

It is not a sexual love - it's the love of caring for people who've had an impact in one's life and the memories of them, i.e. they can always count on me. My love for my wife is both a sexual and emotional one, meaning I am at peace in her presence and totally honest with her. That contentment is what I define as "True Love."

Rachel's take:

"We grow up bombarded with fairy tales and ideals of beauty, roles and behavior: Beauty and the Beast, Cinderella and the heroic and handsome man carting off his blushing bride to the dream land of happily ever after. Boys are encouraged to be "manly" and spend their years in gyms taking steroids to get the body image they think women desire, only to flop miserably in the bedroom once they get into a relationship: I'm speaking from experience here.

Girls fall into the trap too – we get artificial boobs and Botox treatments to impress men who soon get tired of them and start eyeing "real women." This is the frustration that often leads to cheaters. We also need to think about sex and sensitivity training for our outwardly perfect men and women. "

2.   How do you tell if a Love is genuine or not?

Trust your feelings. When I first met Rachel, we just clicked. I think we need to trust our senses more and not worry about what other people may think; it's a gut reaction. If you genuinely want to spend time with somebody without sex being involved then Love is in the air.

Rachel's take:

Their vulnerability - On our first date he told me about all his sexual misadventures and then he cried in public! I kept thinking this is a man seeking another chance and desperate to prove his love.

3.   Is your partner cheating on you and if Yes, should you also cheat?

If one is betrayed then one has the freedom to do the same, however I think cheating is an indication of something being wrong in the relationship and unless that is resolved, one is best off leaving. I totally agreed with Cassandra leaving me after I cheated on her – being angry and drunk is never an excuse, issues need to be sensibly resolved

Rachel's take:

There's a chapter in the book where it talks about meeting partners in a pub – I think that is true because if our first experiences are based on lust alone, what happens down the line when hidden truths and lies emerge? Any relationship based on a lie will ultimately end in tears hence the need for total honesty in the beginning.

4.   Are Orgasms overrated?

The whole point of engaging in sex in the first place is to achieve an Orgasm: it is important for men to understand that when it comes to pleasing women. See to your lady's pleasure first guys and the rest is a no brainer.

Rachel's take:

"No comment; I am happy."

5.   Is love possible without Sex?

The simple answer is Yes. There are varying degrees of love as explained above, however emotional love will always trump sexual love in my experience: get to know and understand someone first before you have sex if you want your love to last.

6.	Can you be in Love with several partners?

It's possible once you learn to differentiate between Emotional and Sexual love. I had a sexual love with all my exe's and we remain friends, however I now share both an emotional and sexual love with my wife stronger than my bonds with anyone. In my Wolf years I experienced sex with different women but there was no "love" involved; it was purely a physical thing. I believe Love is both a conscious and emotional decision.

Rachel's take:

Deep down I know he's still conflicted but tantra helps and he's still a work in progress. I know he believes in multiple love but really, it's guilt he needs to overcome.

8.	Where exactly is the mythical "G" spot and what do you do once it's discovered?

Okay listen very closely students:
Gently place your left hand on where your lover's bladder is located, just above her hip bone.

Lick two fingers and inserting them into her vagina, gently feel around until you feel a difference in the texture – it will feel a little bumpier than the smooth feel of the rest of her vagina. Watch your lady friends face and breathing for changes as you do this – she'll stiffen up slightly or curl her toes once you find the right spot. Rub it gently with your two fingers by using a "come here" motion – keep your other hand on her belly but do not push down on it – you can rub it gently too. For maximum effect gently flick your tongue on her clitoris while rubbing her clitoris.

9.   And finally, the answer to the age-old question "What are you thinking?" (It's never what you think.)

Okay ladies (please forgive me for simply being the messenger here):

A man with a far-off expression is simply one who has sub-consciously tuned you out because to put it delicately, you're simply talking too much and he's afraid to mention it for fear of disrupting the relationship. This has absolutely nothing to do with you or how he feels about you - it's just that our attention spans are not as long as that of women and so our minds tend to wander.
Sorry but it's the truth – we still love you, we'd just prefer to cuddle in silence when a game is on.

Sex Crumbs

I've met and dated some incredible and wonderful ladies in my quest for true love – a veritable male slut who enjoys pleasing women and was always looking for a true relationship but was taken advantage of and so disappointed, reverted to "type."

The honest truth is a naked and willing woman will almost always win over morals; it's the nature of human desire. I have been to the dark side and will hold my head up amidst the hypocrites who fornicate in secret and pretend to have morals in polite society – at our very cores we're all mostly fueled by raw lust: we either learn to control it or it end up controlling us.

My lessons have included heartbreak, depression, betrayal, bigamy, lies, and greed but ultimately love did prevail and these then are my insights:

1. The man who lives in the past is flirting with sorrow – one needs to "move on."

2. Only by losing sight of land does one discover the stars: get out of your comfort zone and seek new vistas if you're unhappy.

3. All that matters in the end is the willingness to simply try again regardless of any hurt or pain we may experience: we only learn and mature through our mistakes.

4. You don't need to be a super hero to get the girl; the right girl will bring out the superhero in you.

5. Love is not about gifts and presents: Love is about the moments spent together and the memories made: that is the greatest treasure of all.

6. The simplest secret of happiness, is wanting what you have.

7. Take a new look at your partner and give them a long & warm hug and think: an intelligent and beautiful human being settled for you despite all your quarks, insecurities and flaws.

And that my friends, is "True Love" – Simple
and Honest Devotion.

The Last Ride Together

"What if we still ride on, we two

With life for ever old yet new,

Changed not in kind but in degree,

The instant made eternity, -

And heaven just prove that I and She

Ride, ride together, for ever ride?"

Robert Browning

This book is a dedication to all the women in
our lives - May we be worthy of them.

Carpe' Diem.

London, 06/2022